KT-389-820

HOPSCOTCH MYTHS

No Dinner for Anansi

by Trish Cooke and Emma Shaw Smith

FRANKLIN WATTS
LONDON•SYDNEY

HOPSCOTCH
MYTHS

No Dinner
for Anansi

ST.HELENS LIBRARIES

3 8055 01355 3094

First published in 2008 by
Franklin Watts
338 Euston Road
London
NW1 3BH

Franklin Watts Australia
Level 17/207 Kent Street
Sydney
NSW 2000

ST HELENS
LIBRARIES

380551355309

Bertrams   29/07/2009

                £3.99

Text © Trish Cooke 2008
Illustration © Emma Shaw Smith 2008

The rights of Trish Cooke to be identified as the author
and Emma Shaw Smith as the illustrator of this Work have
been asserted in accordance with the Copyright, Designs
and Patents Act, 1988.

All rights reserved. No part of this publication may be
reproduced, stored in a retrieval system, or transmitted
in any form or by any means, electronic, mechanical,
photocopy, recording or otherwise, without the prior
written permission of the copyright owner.

A CIP catalogue record for this book is available
from the British Library.

ISBN 978 0 7496 7998 9 (hbk)
ISBN 978 0 7496 8006 0 (pbk)

Series Editor: Melanie Palmer
Series Advisor: Dr Barrie Wade
Series Designer: Peter Scoulding

Printed in China

Franklin Watts is a division of
Hachette Children's Books,
an Hachette Livre UK company
www.hachettechildrens.co.uk

SCHOOLS LIBRARY SERVICE
HORACE ST. LIBRARY
TEL 677806. FAX 677807

Long ago in Africa there lived a
naughty spider called Anansi.

Anansi often ate dinner at other people's homes, but he never invited anyone to eat at his home.

One day, Anansi was cooking
a big dinner for himself when
there was a knock at the door.

"Hello, hello! It's me, Turtle!" called Turtle. "Mmm, that smells like a tasty dinner, Anansi!"

"Come in, Turtle," groaned Anansi. "You're just in time for dinner," he sighed, knowing he would now have to share it.

But as Turtle was about to sit
down, Anansi had an idea.

"Wait! Wait! Your hands are dirty
Turtle, you'd better wash them
before you eat," he said.

"Oh, OK," said Turtle.

Turtle had to go all the way back to the river to wash his hands.

It was a long, long way.

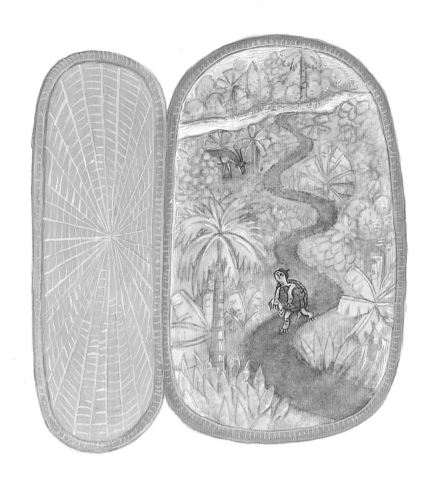

While Turtle was gone, Anansi gobbled up the big dinner all by himself. "Yum, yum, yum! All for me and none for Turtle!" he sang.

When Turtle returned, all the plates were empty. "Never mind," said Turtle, "come to my house for dinner tomorrow!"

"Lovely," said Anansi greedily, "Yum, yum, yum, I can't wait!"

Next day, Anansi went to meet

Turtle at the river bank.

"So where is the dinner you promised me?" Anansi asked, rubbing his belly.

21

"It's on my kitchen table,"
said Turtle, "come on!"

Turtle lived way down at the bottom of the river. So Anansi followed Turtle into the water ...

... but, when Anansi dived in, he kept bobbing on top of the water.

"Hmm," thought Anansi, "I need something to make me sink!"

Anansi found some heavy stones on the river bank and put them in his pockets.

Then he dived back into the water and sank down to the bottom of the river.

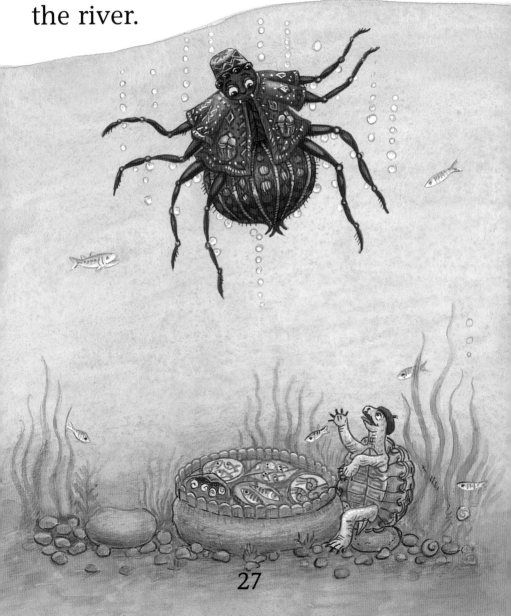

Anansi couldn't wait to tuck
into the lovely dinner, but just
as Anansi was about to start
eating, Turtle shouted,

28

"Wait! Wait! You can't eat
with your jacket on Anansi,
you'd better take it off."
"Oh, OK!" said Anansi.

But as soon as Anansi took his jacket off, he floated straight up to the top of the water!

"Ha, ha! No dinner for you Anansi!" Turtle laughed.

Hopscotch has been specially designed to fit the requirements of the Literacy Framework. It offers real books by top authors and illustrators for children developing their reading skills. There are 63 Hopscotch stories to choose from:

* hardback